PEARL

of Christian Counsel
for the Brokenhearted

by Vernard Eller

calligraphy by Rosanna Eller

UNIVERSITY
PRESS OF
AMERICA

Copyright © 1983 by

University Press of America, Inc.

P.O. Box 19101, Washington, D.C. 20036

Library of Congress Cataloging in Publication Data

Pearl (Middle English poem). English.
  Pearl of Christian counsel for the brokenhearted.

  I. Eller, Vernard. II. Eller, Rosanna. III. Title.
PR2111.A234 1982   821'.1   82-20028
ISBN 0-8191-2850-3
ISBN 0-8191-2851-1 (pbk.)

to
My Pearl

my grandmother, Jessie Pearl

my aunt, Emily Pearl

my sister, Elfreda Pearl

my sister-in-law, Margaret
(from the French for "pearl")

and the remainder of the string not so named:

my other grandmother and aunts,
my mother and mother-in-law,
my wife and daughter,
my other sister-in-laws, nieces, et al.

"so comely a pack of jolly jewels"
(as the poet has it)

acknowledgements

Because, with University Press of America, the author supplies camera-ready copy to the publisher, this book has afforded me some unique opportunities and also necessitated my calling for some unique kinds of help. In addition to being author, I was privileged to be editor, designer, copyeditor, typesetter, proofreader, and more.

All the "elegance" of this book's format is to be credited to the calligraphic art of my own Pearl Maiden (who is actually a **rose**), college-age daughter Rosanna. As in the counterpart relationship within the poem, she is her father's pride and joy. Yet also as within the poem, in the progress of the work she managed to give her dear daddy a real hard time. As the poet so well expresses it, "My bliss and bale—ye have been both!"

Also here in La Verne, two good friends—both professional teachers of design and printing—have helped in creating the book's concept and in preparing the copy for camera. They are Charles E. Davis and Eugene Carper. Their contributions have been invaluable.

And I would be remiss not to mention my word-processing computer, which enabled the not-very-good typesetter (namely, me) to satisfy the perfectionist demands of the proofreader (also me). My thanks to all of the above—and to UPA for having taken over from that point.

--VERNARD ELLER
La Verne CA
Summer 1982

contents

the counsel

HOW ARE WE to cope with loss? What counsel has the Christian gospel for the brokenhearted, what comfort for our grief?

I suppose there is no topic upon which more books are being written in our day—particularly if "loss" be understood broadly as including not only the death of a loved one but also the loss of a marriage, of friendship, of health, of status, of employment, of financial security, of one's youth, of happiness. Many of these books take the form of personal testimony: "This is how it was in my situation. This is how God helped me." And the case will be no different here.

Yet, even in the face of all that has been and is being written, there is room for this book—there is **need** for this book.

The difficulty with other books is that they have been written by contemporaries and so tend to reflect the bias of our day, the bias of current psychological counseling and the gospel as interpreted by that psychology. Conversely, the advantage of this book is that it stands at a distance; six hundred years seems about right for escaping the influences of modernity. Perhaps the change of perspective can give us some fresh insights.

Christians, above all people, should know that the latest is not necessarily the truest. Indeed, the norm of our faith lies in a revelation given almost two thousand years ago, preserved in documents of strange and antique tongue. And closer to the instance of this book, we have an ancient church tradition that includes classics of devotion and counsel, written by saintly teachers and prophets—no people more capable of speaking the word we need to hear.

Yet, for the most part, their word goes unheard and unheeded, because their writings remain untranslated, inaccessible, unpromoted, unknown. This book, then, is the effort to rescue one of these silenced voices and enable one such teacher to impart his counsel to the audience and for the purpose he intended--namely, to his brothers and sisters in Christ for the comfort of their brokenheartedness.

PEARL IS a 14th-century poem known only to students of English literature--if to them. (I was at university in a graduate course on medieval literature before I discovered it.) It is written in English--although not so you could read it. During six hundred years the language has changed perhaps even more than have our intellectual biases. The poem has come down to us in a single manuscript copy, currently housed in the British Museum. This original uses many strange words (strange to us, that is) and even some letters that are no longer in our alphabet. It stands without any sort of punctuation--except for a capital letter at the beginning of each canto. It bears neither a title for the work nor a name for the author. It is bound together with several other poems which likely are by the same poet.

For obvious reasons, the work has come to be known as **Pearl** and the poet (for lack of any other identification) as the Pearl Poet. The poem currently is in print, available in two or three different translations. However, these editions all present it as a specimen for literary analysis; this one as a valuable word of Christian counsel for the brokenhearted. Even so, the translation offered here makes no pretense of putting the poem into modern English. I have changed it only enough to get it within the understanding range of a modern reader--bringing it forward, say, to the language of the King James Bible or Shakespeare. I consider it most important that we read **Pearl** for what it is, a word spoken to our day by an elder (a much elder) brother. (See the Appendix for a more technical discussion of the translation.)

THAT THE LANGUAGE of this writer is different will be obvious. That his **message** is different I think lies in this: The primary assumption behind many contemporary presentations of the gospel--and particularly those intended for grief counseling--is that God and I share a common goal, namely that I be happy and self-accepting. As sufferer, I **know** this is my primary concern; and the church assures me it is God's as well. The conservative church likes to talk about the miraculous blessings he is just waiting to heap

upon me, and the liberal church prefers to focus upon the
psychological therapies and social arrangements that are
his vehicles for helping me feel better; but the church is
united in approving my pursuit of happiness and telling me
of God's support in the matter. Yet, on the contrary,
the Pearl Poet specifically raises the question of whether
any true, Christian comfort is to be found that way. His
counsel is different.

canto 1

Pearl, pleasant to a prince's pleasure,
To cleanly enclose in gold so clear,
Out of the Orient, I boldly say,
None ever proved her precious peer.
So round, so right in each array,
So small, so smooth her sleek sides were;
Whenever I judged gems so gay
I set her singly in singularity.
Alas! I lost her in an herb garden
Through grass to ground it from me got!
I dwindled, done in by love-distress
For that prize pearl without a spot.

LET US BEGIN by noting some features of the poem that, in varying degree, are preserved in the translation before us.

The one thing no translation can preserve is the **sound** of the original. Many even of the poet's words that we could recognize visually have changed enough in pronunciation that the "sound" of the poetry is entirely different for us from what it was for him. I wish you could "hear" the Pearl Poet; but only experts in historical linguistics are competent to do an oral performance of the work.

The original poem does have a more or less regular **meter.** Our translation comes down rather more on the less side, but enough is preserved that you can tell what the meter is supposed to be—namely, four stresses per line.

The original has a strict **rhyme scheme** with every line rhyming one way or another. The translation is forced to break the pattern time after time. But again, enough has been preserved for you to hear the rhyme and know where it should be. (Eight of the twelve lines in this first stanza are according to scheme.)

A prominent feature of the original is the use of **alliteration,** i.e. the repeating of a particular sound throughout a line by using a number of words that begin with (or stress) the same letter. I have taken great pains to retain the alliteration in this translation.

A key structural feature of **Pearl** is its **linkage.** The poet accomplishes this with what we shall call **catch lines** and **link words.** The pattern will become evident as we proceed, but it is constructed thus: A canto is a sequence of five stanzas. Beginning with the final line of the first stanza of a canto and running through the first line of the first stanza of the succeeding canto, the first and the final lines of each stanza are "catch lines" which include the "link word" for that canto. As our first instance, the link word of Canto I is "spot."

Particularly striking—although the full significance will not come to us until the very end of the poem—is the fact that the very first line of the poem is a catch line of the final canto, No. XX. This neatly is the poem's end linked to its beginning and the whole made into a beautiful unity. Along the way, each canto is linked to its successor by the same device.

IF YOU HAVE NOT guessed it from this first stanza, it will soon become apparent that the speaker actually is describing the death of a baby girl (not yet two years old, we are told later) who was close to him—presumably his daughter.

The herb garden is, of course, the graveyard. It is possible, I suppose, that the baby was even named "Pearl"—or more likely "Margery" [from the French word for pearl, "margarite"]—although this can be only conjecture.

However, it is likely, here at the outset, that the poet wants us to be reminded of Jesus' parable about the pearl of great price (Mt. 13:45-46)—to which he will make explicit reference later. One lesson the father will have to learn is that he was wrong in taking even his beloved daughter as being the pearl of great price. No, only the kingdom of God—his sovereign rule—is the pearl to be sought before, and at the cost of, everything else. As long as my own happiness (or that in which I find my happiness) is put first, Christianity can offer no sure and lasting comfort.

IT CERTAINLY IS possible that the poem is autobiographical, that the poet actually did lose a daughter and, in consequence, experience the revelation he describes. Yet perhaps we ought not take that for granted. In any case, we will need to make the distinction between the person who wrote the poem and the one who is both the first-person speaker of it and a character within it. Even if it should be that the poem is autobiographical and the two men the same, the difference of perspective between writing the account of an experience after it is all over and being right in the middle of it is one well worth maintaining. Accordingly, the person of the first situation we shall refer to as "the poet" (the Pearl Poet). And on the other hand, the father who is telling the story does on occasion refer to himself as "the Jeweler"; so let us use that term to identify him.

The implication attending the term "Jeweler" (who "judges gems so gay," setting her "singly in singularity") is that of person who is considered by others and who considers himself competent to make a true evaluation of jewels. Consequently, the issue of the poem—for him and for us—is whether he and we **do** prove to be truly "gentle Jewelers" in picking our pearl of great price.

I:2

Since, in the spot it from me sprung,
Oft have I waited, wishing that weal
That was wont for a while to void my wrong
And heighten my happiness and all
                              my health—
Though now hurt thru my heart doth throng,
While my breast doth bulge and burn
                              in bale.

Yet thought me ne'er was so sweet a song
As such a still stand let to me steal;
Forsooth, not a few I did there feel,
To think of her color now clad in clot.
O mold, thou marrest a merry jewel,
My priceless pearl without a spot.

NOTICE THE LINK WORD "spot" in both the first and the last lines of the stanza.

The Jeweler makes it plain how completely his life had come to center in that baby girl. ("Certainly there is nothing wrong in that! . . . Is there?") He gives—and will give—eloquent expression to the terrible pain her loss has brought. He is being honest; and such pain can arouse in us nothing but sympathy.

"Yet thought me ne'er was so **sweet** a song." Is that true? It is; and the poet is on to something very important.

Unless redeemed in the will of God, grief is bound to become a very self-centered (even self-centering) emotion. **My** loss doth thrust **my** heart through. I am hurting in a way which ought to command the attention and sympathy of everyone around. Grief thus affords me an opportunity for some self-indulgence that no one would dare to find blameworthy. And there is a certain "sweetness" in that. The poet has alerted us: grief can seduce us into loving it, even while we are hurting under it.

That spot with spices needs must spread,
Where such riches to rot have run;
Blooms blond and blue and red
Shall shine full sheer against the sun.
Flower and fruit cannot there fail,
Where it down into the dark was done;
For each grass from a dead grain must grow,
Else no wheat were for warehouses won.
Of good each good is ever begun!
With so seemly a seed it could fail not
That sprigs of spices up have sprung
From that precious pearl without a spot.

HERE THE JEWELER sees a truth that could have been of great help to him—if only he could have held to it (which, we will see, he did not do). Yet such is **grief**: our pain makes us deaf to the truth, whether it be something told us by a loving counselor or even something we tell ourselves.

The truth, in this instance, is the faith that goodness ultimately is indestructible. Or, better put: "We know that in everything God works for good with those who love him" (Rom. 8:28). "**Of** good each good is ever begun." The good God accomplished even through the death of his only Son enables Christians to believe that—indeed, it forbids us to believe anything else.

Granted, the Jeweler, in the face of his grief, was not able to keep on believing. Granted, we find it difficult to keep on believing in our turn. Yet that does not stop the thought from being the very truth of things in any case.

I:4

To that spot I in speech expound,
I entered, there in that garden green,
In August, in a high season
When corn is cut with sickles keen.
On the hill the pearl had trundled down,
Were shadowed these shrubs, sheer and
                                    shining:
Gillyflower, ginger, and gromwell,
With peonies powdered all between.
Though seemly a scene simply to be seen,
A fair fragrance as well floated from the plot.
There waits worthily, I ween,
My precious pearl without a spot.

I:5

Upon that spot my hands I'd wring
For care, full cold, that at me caught;
A desolate dirge in my heart did din,
Though to set me right my reason sought.
I made plaint for my pearl that was
                              pent therein,
With ferocious feelings that fast me fought.
Though Christ's character could my comfort
                              have been,
My wretched will in woe was wrought
As I fell on that field with flowers fraught.
Then such odor to my senses shot
Sleep slipped o'er me in its onslaught
Near that precious pearl without a spot.

TRULY, GRIEF IS a seducer in more ways than one. It is not that no word of comfort is being spoken but that grief's desolate dirge can set us against reason itself and even drown out the comfort Christ would offer. The difficulty, of course, is that--although later the Jeweler would come to see what grief was and what it had done to him--in the moment his wretched will prevented him from seeing anything. And so with us; yet perhaps the poet's describing it **now** can alert us to the situation **then**, when we are the ones blinded by grief.

canto 11

From that spot my spirit sprang into
                         space;
My body on the berm there 'bode in dreaming.
My ghost is gone, in God's good grace,
Upon adventure of marvelous meaning.
I wist not where in this world my place;
But I knew I'd been cast near climbing
                            cliffs.

Toward a forest then I fixed my face
Where rich rocks there I did perceive.
The light from them you'd not believe
Their gleaming glory did so glint
For never were webs that women weave
Of half so dear adornment.

AS WE ENTER a new canto,   notice how the catch line   opening this   first   stanza uses   the   link word, "spot,"   from   the previous   canto,   whereas the   concluding catch line   intro- duces a new link word, "adornment" or "adorned."

The   poet's word "ghost"   in the   third line   would, of course,   normally translate into our   word "soul," or "spir- it."   But   to go modern would be to efface a beautiful piece of   alliteration; so   understand   "ghost" according   to   the poet's meaning rather than ours.

Adorned those downs were on every side
With crystal cliffs so clear in kind.
Forests bright 'bout them stood betide
With boles in indigo blue outlined.
Like burnished silver the leaves did slide
That trembled thickly where they twined.
The gleam of the glade 'gainst them did glide,
With shimmering sheen full sharp they
shined.
The gravel that on the ground did grind
Was precious pearls of Orient;
The sunbeams were but blank and blind
In respect of that adornment.

II : 3

The adornment of those downs so dear
Engendered my ghost all grief to forget.
Of such fresh flavors the fruits were,
As food they would me fairly surfeit.
Fowls there flew thru the forest in flocks,
Of flambouyant hues, both small and great;
But citole string and gittern player
Their reckless mirth cannot repeat,
For when these birds their wings did beat
They sang so, with a sweet assent.
More gracious glee could no one get
Than to hear and see this adornment.

II : 4

Dearly adorned I it all did apprise
In the forest where fortune had
fared me forth.
The dazzle thereof for to devise
In way of words is nothing worth.
I then walked out in well-feeling wise
No bank so big but it gave me berth.
The farther in the forest, the fairer did rise
The plain, the plants, the spice, the pears,
And rows and ridges and also rich rivers
As filaments fine their banks were bent.
I wound to a water that past a shore swerves
Lord, dear was its adornment!

II : 5

The adornments of that darkling deep
Were beautiful banks of beryl bright.
Swirling sweetly the water did sweep;
With rumbling roar it went racing aright.
Out in the flood there stood stones so steep,
Gleaming as tho' they with glass were bedight
As streaming stars do while stragglers sleep,
Swarmed in the welkin of cold winter night.
For an emerald, sapphire, or jewel bright
Was each of the pebbles in that pool pent,

Limning all the loch with its light,
So dear was its adornment.

canto III

The adornment dear of down and dales,
Of wood and water and widening plain,
Built in me bliss, abated my wails,
Dispelled my distress, and destroyed my pain.
Down after a stream that unfailingly flows
I bent my way blissfully ~ brim full my
                                          brain.
The further I followed those flocculent vales
The stronger the joy my heart did contain.
Thus Fortune fares with whomever she'd
                                          train:
Whether solace she sends or else sorrow sore,
The wight who to her will is fain
Is bound to have ever more and more.

OUR POET DELIGHTS in the visual imagery of beauty and glory; and he is an artist in his use of it.

His thought at the conclusion of this stanza is an important one. Grief does tend to feed upon itself and bring us into further grief. Just so, joy tends to create more of itself, leading us on from joy to joy. The Jeweler, now, has experienced both cycles. The lesson, I think, is that we be alerted to this characteristic of grief and thus resist being sucked into its undertow.

If you have not yet figured out where the Jeweler is, he will figure it out for himself in the next stanza. Give close attention to what he has to say about the river; it is to become one of his central symbols. The river itself is a familiar one, although the Jeweler never names it. Three hundred years later, Christian--in **The Pilgrim's Progress**--will encounter some difficulty in crossing this same stream, although, again, without naming it. Then, after a couple more centuries, out of an entirely different land and culture, the "deep river" will be named "Jordan." Yet the Jeweler is at one with that singer in wanting to "cross over into camp ground."

III : 2

More of weal there was in that wise
Than I could tell if time I had,
For earthly heart may not suffice
To the tenth part of such gladness glad.
Therefore thought I that Paradise
Beyond the stream's bank was there to be had;
I hoped the water was a device
Dividing mirths by measure made.
Beyond the brook, by glen or glade,
I hoped to mark a mighty manor.
But the water was deep; I durst not wade.
And ever I longed ~ aye more and more.

III : 3

More and more and yet still more
I longed the brook to see beyond;
For if 'twas fair where I could fare,
Much lovelier was that farther land.
About me I did stand and stare.
Fast to find a ford I planned;
But many impasses indeed were there
The further I walked along the strand.
Yet I'd not myself bring to a stand,
Fearing weals to be won were yet in store.
Then I noticed something had come to hand
That moved my mind e'er more and more.

III : 4

More marvels did my sense assault !
I saw beyond that merry mere
A crystal cliff full relucent;
Many royal a ray did from it rear.
At the foot thereof sat an infant,
A maiden majestic, full debonair;
And vestally white was her vesture.
I knew her well; I had seen her ere !
As glistening gold that men shave sheer,
So shone she shining on other shore.
At length I looked upon her there
The longer, I knew her more and more.

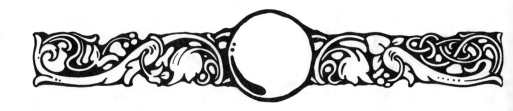

YES, YOU HAVE correctly identified the "maiden majestic"; but the poet's word "infant" is not quite the give-away you might think. In his day, "infant" covered a much broader age-range than it does for us. Thus the "infantry" consisted of troops too young and inexperienced for the cavalry.

III : 5

The more I fathomed the fair face
Of this fine figure I had found,
Such gladdening glory did me grace
As not long before had been my wont.
The desire to call her did me embrace;
But bewilderment gave my heart a brunt
I saw her in so strange a place,
Such a burst might my heart benumb!
Then she toward me raised her fair front,
Her visage white as ivory pure.
It stung my heart, me straightway
                              stunned
And ever the longer, more and more.

canto iv

More than I wished, my dread arose;
I stood full still and durst not call.
With eyes wide ope and mouth full closed
I stood there heedful as hawk in hall.
I guessed ghostly purpose was proposed
And was in dread what should befall,
Lest she escape whom I saw disclosed.
While I, to salute her, was forestalled,
That gracious gay one without gall,
So smooth, so small, so seemly slight,
Rose up in her array royale,
A precious piece in pearls bedight.

IV : 2

Bedight with pearls of royal price,
There could by grace her charm be read
When she, fresh as a fleur-de-lis,
Bent down the bank her steps bestead.
Of virgin white were her vestments,
Open at sides and beautifully spread
With the merriest margarites, to my mind,
On which my eyes had ever fed
With large laps of linen, too, I ween,
Decked with double pearl so bright.
Her kirtle, in the self-same scheme,
With precious pearls was all bedight.

IV : 3

A coronet yet bedight that girl,
Of margarites and no other stone,
High pinnacled of clear white pearl,
With perfect flower figures thereon;
No ornament else 'bout her head did curl.
Her gracious gaze met all and one,
Her semblance staid as duke or earl's
Her blush more bonny than whalebone.
Like gold shaved sheer her hair then shone,
On her shoulders lying loose and light.
And her deep collar wanted none,
A border ⌐'twas with pearls bedight.

: IV : 4

Bedight, too, were cuffs and hem,
At hands, at sides, at aperture,
With pearl of white, no other gem;
And burnished white was her vesture.
Yet a wondrous pearl without weakness
Between her breasts was set so sure;
A man's assay must surely cease
Before his mind masters its measure.
I guess there's no tongue could endure
Not to speak salutary of that sight,
It was so clean and clear and pure
That precious pearl which her bedight.

NOTICE, here and following, both through imagery and explicit statement, how high a value our poet puts upon **purity.** "Purity," for him, obviously pertains to things sexual but to much else as well. Then consider that we live in a society where "purity" has become an impossible concept, if not a ridiculous one. For us, "purity" must mean "puritanism" and signifies only that a person has denied himself all sorts of pleasures, with nothing gained in consequence.

Perhaps if we gave more attention to "purity," we would be more successful in finding the "comfort" we so zealously seek. The two concepts are not unrelated—at least not in the revelation of this poet.

IV:5

Bedight in pearl, that precious piece
Across the water came down the shore.
No one gladder from here to Greece
Than I when toward the brim she bore.
She was nearer me than aunt or niece;
My joy, therefore, was much the more.
She proffered speech, that special grace,
Inclining low, me to implore,
Cast off the crown that she had worn,
And lifted her voice in language light.
Well 'twas for me that I was born
To answer that angel in pearls bedight.

canto v

"O Pearl," quod I, "in pearls bedight,
Art thou my pearl that hast me pained,
Caused me to grieve alone at night?
Much longing for thee have I maintained
Since in the grass thou didst alight.
Pensive and pallid, I'm profaned,
Whilst thou, in life of liking light,
Art in Paradiseland with strife
                             unstained.
What fate hath hither my jewel constrained
And me put into distress and danger?
Since we in twain were torn and taken,
I've been a joyless jeweler."

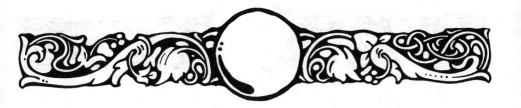

V:2

That jewel then in gentle gems
Veered up her face with eyes of gray,
Put on her crown of orient pearl,
And after that didst soberly say:
"Sir, you your tale have taken amiss,
To say your pearl is all away,
Which in a coffer so comely is closed
As in this garden gracious and gay,
Herein to dwell forever and play,
Where mishap or mourning never come near.
Here were a jewel box for thee, in fay,
If thou wert a gentle jeweler.

V:3

"But, gentle jeweler, if thou shalt lose
Thy joy for a gem that to thee was so dear,
Methinks thou art put to a mad purpose
And busieth thyself without reason clear;
For what thou didst lose was but a rose
That flowered and failed as all such
turn sear.

Now, thru the kind of chest doth it enclose,
As a true pearl of price it's been proven here.
Thou takest thy fate as a thing to fear,
Tho naught's been made aught for thee,
as 'twere.

Thou blamest the balm for thy disease so drear;
Thou art no gentle jeweler!"

HERE, with the maiden's first words to the Jeweler, we encounter what will be a continuing theme and, I suggest, the
distinctive contribution of the poem as a whole. Let's
consider it in some depth before letting the poet take it
from there.

The father, full of the anguish of his bereavement,
suddenly finds his lost daughter. More, she can now speak
to him in the voice of heaven itself. The comfort he so
needs and has so sought is at hand. In all sincerity and
innocence he expresses to her his heartfelt condition. And
she **scolds him but good**—and will continue to do so in
stanza after stanza. His response is what ours would be:
"How can you talk that way? Can't you see I'm hurting?"
The poet is revealing some of the hidden assumptions that
regularly underlie our own grief feelings.

In the first place, as was suggested earlier, grief of
itself can be a very self-centered and self-centering emotion. When we are in the throes, it is hard to see anything except our own desperate need. Other concerns and
other people with their concerns simply cease to exist.
The maiden puts it bluntly: "You aren't mourning **me**; there
is nothing about **my** condition that calls for mourning.
Indeed, contemplation of my situation could be a balm to
you. No, you are mourning (feeling sorry for) yourself;
you are lamenting only your own grief and pain. Your ho-
rizon has become constricted to the desire for your own
happiness."

Despite his own protestations otherwise, the upshot
shows that it was not for itself the Jeweler valued "the
peerless pearl" (whose beauty has now been immeasurably
enhanced). Rather, he valued it for the enjoyment **he** de-
rived from its possession—a consideration of an entirely
different order.

In the second place, grief has the effect of impress-
ing us with our own innocence. "For me to hurt this much
has got to be unfair; I couldn't have done anything to deserve **this!**" In grief, I know myself to be "poor me"; and
I feel very strongly that other people should recognize me
that way as well.

In such case, if we do look for **sin** ("What did I do
wrong?"), we usually look in the wrong place. Certainly
the poem nowhere suggests that the Jeweler had done anything that moved God to punish him by taking his daughter.
No more had the biblical Job done anything to deserve his
immeasurable loss. Yet both men had to repent of sin—the
sin of grieving the way they did; of making the desire for
their own consolation their only priority in life; of
shutting out the possibility that God might have a purpose
that **included** their suffering, a plan that went beyond

simply getting them comforted at the earliest possible moment.

Still, in grief, it is as much as impossible for us to understand the grief itself as being **sin**. "Do you think I **want** to be grieving? Do you think I **chose** to feel this way? Don't you think I would be glad to feel otherwise if I could find any way of doing so?" Yet be that as it may, the gospel is not as impressed with our innocence as we are.

The third assumption lying behind much of our grief is the one to which the poem gives most attention. Certain of our own innocence, we proceed to invent the rather illogical equation that **suffering** somehow comes to count as **merit**. Because I have suffered, I now **deserve** special treatment. "How can you talk to me that way? Can't you see I'm hurting?"

We even have a common idiom for expressing the idea: "He's suffered enough already." Now in many cases that may well be so; and if the implied next line is, "So quit picking on him," it's a good word. However, if, as seems more likely, the implied next line is, "Therefore he now **deserves** surcease, comfort, and joy," it does not follow. No, it is not my place to lay suffering upon any other individual; but neither am I called to make the judgment as to what constitutes enough in any situation.

Recall what the writer to the Hebrews tells us, that even Jesus "learned obedience through what he suffered" (5:8). So if it should be that God has in mind for us a lesson to be learned through suffering and we haven't learned it yet, then manifestly it is not true that "we have suffered enough already." And anyway, it plainly is not the case that our suffering puts God under obligation to make it up to us with a commensurate reward.

AND SO THE MAIDEN of heavenly vision rises up to chastize her poor, grief-stricken, dear daddy. Yet we should know that this is not the first time such a story has taken so startling and seemingly inappropriate a turn. In the Bible are two works that speak in a special way to the topic before us: the writings of the prophet Jeremiah and the book of Job. Because Jeremiah's is a personal testimony right out of the midst of his suffering, it may be the more powerful.

Jeremiah lived through a very rough time; and his personal fortunes reflected the agony of the nation itself. Jerusalem was beseiged by (eventually to fall to) Babylonian armies. God directed the prophet to advocate surrender. In consequence, everyone turned against him. God forbade him to take a wife and have a family. His friends and relatives shunned him; and some of them even plotted his assassination. In his misery Jeremiah turned to God, feeling that, under the circumstances, a little comfort wasn't too much to ask. And God's response?

> If you have raced with men and the runners
>   have worn you down,
> how then can you hope to vie with horses?
> If you fall headlong in easy country,
> how will you fare in Jordan's dense thickets?
>   (Jeremiah 12:5 NEB)

"Sorry, my friend, but you have **not** suffered enough already!"

It was not, of course, that God enjoyed being cruel or that he had forgotten Jeremiah or stopped loving him. In time, the prophet came to realize that--which realization itself bore fruit in a very pointed accusation against the social leaders of the time:

> They have healed the wound of my people lightly,
>   saying, "Peace, peace,"
> when there is no peace.
>   (Jeremiah 6:14 NEB)

It could be that the charge catches the counselors of our day even more than those of Jeremiah's. The prophet apparently was referring to the counsel being given regarding the one particular political situation; we have made it the fundamental counsel of both psychology and religion. Whether regarding divorce, promiscuity, deceit, abortion, homosexuality, pornography, you name it, the word is "Peace, peace; there is no evidence here of any wound that needs healing. It is not our business what people do (or what they sell); it is for us to accept them as persons." We have become experts at "healing the wound lightly" (which, of course, is not to heal it at all) saying, "That's all right! That's all right!" when actually it is not right at all.

Whatever the grief or suffering, we are quick to assuage the hurt, telling the person what he wants to hear, giving him the sympathy and stroking he craves (and thinks he **needs**). This to the point that the noted psychiatrist Karl Menninger felt constrained to write a book entitled **Whatever Became of Sin?**

Yet Jeremiah became grateful for the true healing that came from the God who was willing to say, "Sorry, friend, but you have not suffered enough already." And the Jeweler will become grateful that, for his true healing, the maiden was willing to offend by telling him what he decidedly did not want to hear.

Job, too, in the face of total loss, innocently and sincerely turned to God, pleading, praying, begging, bad- gering, demanding that he come and make things right. God eventually came. Did he say, "Poor Job! He's suffered enough already. Now, now, that's all right! We'll make it all well!"? He did not! He said, "Who is this whose ig- norant words cloud my design in darkness? (38:2)"--sounding suspiciously like the Pearl Maiden.

Job had not suffered enough and did not until, at the very end of the book, he was ready to say, "I **repent** in dust and ashes (42:6)." That lesson learned, however, and God immediately became all healing, help, and comfort. Yet consider that, if those adept in healing the wound lightly had gotten to Job first, they would have botched the great healing, the great plan God had in mind for him. How many people in our day, I wonder, have been given "botched com- fort" that left the wound unhealed?

But "repent"? Repent of what? Job repented precisely of what we earlier called the sinful assumptions often ly- ing behind our grieving. He repented of the self-center- edness that kept him from seeing anything except his own need for consolation. He repented that "poor me" had been so convinced of his own innocence that he was blind to the sinfulness of that very attitude. He repented that he had equated suffering with merit and consequently presented God with a bill for services due.

And as Job repented, he made a most interesting ob- servation about himself: "I knew of thee then only by re- port, but now I see thee with my own eyes (42:5)." He **had** known God only by report--the report that he is some sort of Super Santa Claus whom our innocent tears will bring running to make it all well as he pats us on the head and heaps our lap with candy. But **now** Job sees God with his own eyes and understands that God can work larger purposes than Job had ever dreamed--purposes that can include, use, and redeem even our suffering. Thus Job learned the lesson that could be learned only through suffering. Yet, surely, the gain of learning to see God with one's own eyes is well worth any suffering that might be entailed.

YET, ALTHOUGH God's word--"Sorry, but you have not suffered enough already"--**may** be a sign of sin and a call to repen- tance, this is not necessarily the case. We do not know that it was so with Jeremiah; it definitely was not with Jesus.

In the garden, his heart ready to break with grief (as the text has it in Matthew 26:38-39 NEB), he prays, "Father, take this cup away from me"—the same prayer that is prayed by the Jeweler, Jeremiah, Job, and ourselves. The difference is that we stop at that point (with the desire for comfort). Jesus appends a second sentence that takes priority over the first: "Yet not what I will, but what thou wilt." And that does make all the difference, because it recognizes the possibility that the surcease of my suffering may not be the **only** consideration involved. Thus I become open to other priorities, God's priorities.

But the Lord God will not, in the instance of Jesus, heal the wound (humanity's wound) lightly; the cup must be drained. However, it is Dietrich Bonhoeffer who pointed out that this in itself **was** the answer to Jesus' prayer: the cup **could** be taken away, although only by his draining it. Such, in effect, was also God's answer to Jeremiah; and we need always consider that it could as well be God's answer to **our** pleas for comfort.

Yet we should be eternally grateful that, in his extremity, Jesus went to God rather than coming to us. We likely would have said, "Poor Jesus, goodness knows you've suffered enough already; now you certainly deserve something better than death on a nasty old cross"—and the redemption of the world would have been botched.

In a somewhat different case (2 Cor. 12:7-9), the Apostle Paul, nowise guilty, was sure he had suffered enough already and so three times besought the Lord to remove the thorn in the flesh, his "messenger of Satan." But God said (and proceeded to demonstrate), "My grace is sufficient for you, for my power is made perfect in weakness." And Paul undoubtedly valued this lesson more than he would have the cessation of his suffering.

Recall, finally, that, although upon his earthly leave-taking Jesus promised to send the **Comforter**, when that Comforter put in his appearance it was (not unlike the Pearl Maiden) in the form of "tongues as of fire"—a symbol, surely, of something quite different from the sympathy, stroking, and acceptance we define as "comfort."

IN ANOTHER OLD POEM—which, by its own logic, must now be classed uncouth—we are told: "**Time** makes ancient good uncouth." That is true; and of course it holds as well for **Newsweek** and all other pushers of update, downright fact. Undoubtedly our time has made the following analogy untruth as well as uncouth; but I proffer it notwithstanding.

When I was a kid with a cut cuticle, I had a choice. (Actually I didn't; but I always argued that I **should.**) I could have **mercurochrome.** The advantage of mercurochrome was that it didn't hurt and it looked nice (bright pink). The disadvantage was that it was more "chrome" than "cure"; the good it did applied more to the ego than the wound. On the other hand (no; on the **same** hand, but otherwise), I could have **iodine.** Iodine did some good; the trouble was that it stung like fury.

Now God is just like my iodine-loving mother—determined to do what is best for a person no matter how it hurts. When one's problem in the first place is the fact that he's hurting, it doesn't seem quite right just to make him hurt worse. And consequently, we have the word that Jeremiah addresses to **our** generation, saying, "They have healed the wound of my people lightly, saying, 'Mercurochrome by all means! You've suffered enough already.'"

Now, of course, nothing we have said or that the Pearl Poet will say is meant to suggest that Christian comfort always must take this **astringent** aspect and never that of gentleness and balm. Obviously, scripture could provide many examples of the latter. But without at least the possibility of stringency, the healing work of comfort will never be full and true. This is the poet's argument; our discourse has been intended to help **him** make it—and we now allow him to proceed.

V:4

A jewel to me then was this guest,
And jewels her gentle sayings were.
"Indeed," quod I, " my blissful best,
To my distress thou bringest a cure;
To pardoned be I make request.
I thought my pearl was gone for good;
But now it's found, I'll take my rest
And walk with it through the bright wood
And love my Lord as he says I should
Who hath me to this bliss brought near.
Now were I with you beyond this flood,
I'd be a gentle jeweler."

V:5

"Jeweler," said that gem so clean,
"Why jest ye, man? So mad ye be!
Three words at once you've spoken, I ween;
fll-advised, forsooth, they were all three.
Thou wist not what in the world they mean;
Thy words before thy wits do flee.
Thou sayest thou believest me on this scene
Because thou mayest with eyes me see.
And then thou sayest, in this country
Thyself shalt walk with me right here.
The third — to pass this water free —
That may no joyful jeweler.

canto vi

"I hold that jeweler little to praise
Who believeth well what he seeth with eye,
And much to blame and discourteous
Who believeth our Lord would make a lie,
Who loyally promised your life to raise,
Tho fortune destined your flesh to die.
Ye make his words a motley maze
Who nothing believe unless ye it see;
That is a pride unworthy of praise
Which any good man will never
                        indulge

No tale believing as truth he can trace
Except when his own sense is the judge.

REGARDING THIS STANZA, the poet likely thought of John 20:29 before you did. There, upon the Apostle Thomas's becoming convinced through a material manifestation of the risen Lord, Jesus says, "Because you have seen me you have found faith. Happy are they who never saw me and yet have found faith."

Of course, there simply is no Christian faith apart from the willingness to take the Lord at his word, in the absence of demonstrable evidence, refusing to believe that he would make a lie. But the principle has particular relevance to the matter of grief, as the poet himself applies it. Concerning the death of a loved one, if the mourner refuses to believe there is life after death until he "seeth with eye," there is little in the way of hope and comfort that can be afforded him. The maiden is correct; for the Jeweler to say, "Now I believe," is not much of a recommendation of his faith or his being a candidate for Christian comfort. And if modern Christians choose to let stand the implication that their Lord made a lie, what comfort can they expect their "faith" to provide?

Yet the principle also applies more broadly. If, in any sort of grief, I refuse to believe that comfort is possible until I actually can see it, I cut myself off from some of the greatest consolations of the gospel. If I refuse to believe that an experience has any meaning until I can spell out that meaning in terms of my own comprehension, I am bound to miss some of the most valuable lessons there. If I refuse to believe that God works in all things for good until I can locate the good, there are many goods that will never be mine. To believe only "when my own sense is the judge" is not to **believe** at all. And where there is no belief, how is Christian comfort to be found?

VI : 2

"Judge now thyself, whether thou
                        didst not dally,
As tho toward God one's words he should heave.
Thou sayest that thou shalt dwell in this valley;
Methinkest thou first ought to ask leave
And yet might thou fail in getting the grant.
Thou wishest over this water to weave;
But to other counsel must thou consent.
Thy cold corpse must crumble and to
                        the clods cleave,
For corrupted it was at the Paradise trees,
There where our forefather his life misspent.
Each man must drive thru death's dread disease
Ere crossing this stream upon God's judgement.

INTRODUCED HERE is an idea soon to become central. The Jeweler, as a sufferer, has assumed that consolation is his **by right**. Rather than plead for it as a boon, he proposes to **take** it—walk right in, as it were. And then, notice in the next stanza, when she tells him "no," he accuses **her** of being cruel and causing his suffering. Earlier he had admitted that, through grief, he had set himself against reason. Here he's proving it—as do we all.

VI : 3

Quod I, "If thou judgest me, my sweet,
To dole again, then am I deadened.
What I forlost, if I once more greet,
Must I also forego it ere my end?
Why must I it both miss and meet?
My precious pearl with pain doth
                                    me rend.

What serves a treasure except as defeat
If it shall later in trauma be taken?
Now reckless am I how far I decline
Or how far of field men do me send.
When parted from this pearl of mine,
Who can judge that but dole without end?"

VI:4

"Judgest thou naught but of dole-distress?"
Then said that wight, "Why dost thou so?
For din of his dole over lesser losses,
Oft many a man more good doth forego.
Better 'twould be that thou thyself bless
And always love God in weal and in woe,
For anger gaineth thee not a straw;
Who needs must hurt should not be curt.
For tho you're distraught as any doe
Bellow thy brashest, brandish and bray
When thou canst no further, to nor fro,
Thou must by his judgement abide
                              anyway.

"CAN'T YOU THINK of anything except yourself and your own pain?" the Pearl Maiden asks. "You accuse me, and you accuse God. Quit fighting it; your anger won't gain you a straw. In any case, **we** are not tormenting you; you're doing it to yourself."

The poet had the words "thole" and "thro" in place of "hurt" and "curt" (his way fits the rhyme scheme and mine doesn't). But together I think we deserve credit for a real pearl of Christian counsel: "Who needs must hurt should not be curt." Granted, it is hard for us to understand that the manner of our hurting amounts to a being curt with God; but once we do understand and confess it so, there is no doubt but that Christian comfort is at hand.

VI:5

"Judge God; ever him indict ～
He won't place a foot where it doesn't belong.
Thy opinions ∠ don't amount to a mite,
Tho thou, for sorrow, ne'er have a song.
Stop then thy strife and finish thy flight
And seek now his favor full swiftly and strong;
Thy prayer may then move him to pity
                                    thy plight,
That Mercy may with her power respond.
His comfort may with thy capriciousness cope
That thou thy losses no longer begrudge;
For, be moody or mad, mourn and mope,
All lies with him to juggle and judge."

canto vii

Then a judgement made I to that damosel:
"Reckon it not as wrath toward my Lord
If rashly I rave, words tumbling pell-mell;
My heart, as pierced by sorrow's sword,
Gushed weltering water from a well.
I wish his mercy he'd me afford.
So rebuke me not with 𝔏 words so fell,
E'en though I blunder, my dear adored.
But discover to me kindly your comfort,
Pitifully thinking thou upon this:
Of care and me, ye made accord,
Who once was ground of all my bliss.

VII:2

"My bliss, my bale, ye both have been;
But much the more, it was my moan
Since thou wast cast out from my ken
I wist not where my pearl was gone.
Now I see it; now my woe has waned.
When we parted we were at one;
God forbid that we now be wroth
We meet so seldom by stock or stone.
Although courteously ye can carp,
I am but mud and mumble amiss.
But Christ's mercy and Mary and John
These are the ground of all my bliss.

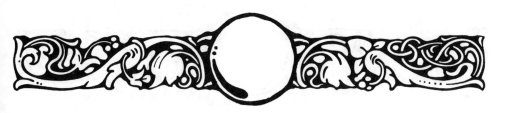

VII:3

"In bliss I see thee blithely blent,
And I a man all mournful made.
Ye take thereof full ⟋ little intent
That I'm hurt oft by harms I hate.
But now that I'm in your presence,
I would beseech without debate
That ye say to me in sober assent
What life ye lead, early and late;
For I'm full fain that your estate
Is altered to such affluence as this.
To all my joy ⟋ the high gate
It is ⌁ and ground of all my bliss."

"Now bliss, beloved, must thee betide!"
That lovely of limb and look spoke clear.
'I welcome thee here to walk and bide,
For now thy speech to me is dear.
Masterful mood and highest pride,
I hint thee, are heatedly hated here.
My Lord loves not at all to chide,
For meek are all who him dwell near.
And when at his place thou shalt appear,
Be deeply devout in holy meekness;
My Lord the Lamb loves aye such cheer,
Who is the ground of all my bliss.

VII : 5

"A blissful life thou sayest I lead;
Thou wouldst thereof then know the stage.
Thou knowest full well, when thy pearl fell,
I was full young and tender of age.
But my Lord the Lamb, thru his Godhead,
He took myself to his marriage,
Crowned me his queen to blossom in bliss
Thru length of days that ne'er shall pass.
And possessed of all his heritage
His beloved is. I'm wholly his!
His poise, his power, his patronage
Are root and ground of all my bliss."

MUCH MORE THAN any sort of visible glories (although the poet already has described many and will describe many more) the Pearl Maiden knows well that it is her personal relationship to Jesus Christ--to his poise, his power, and his patronage--that is the root and ground of all her bliss. The Jeweler, in time, will come to know this, too. Indeed, probably both here and in scripture, the physical imagery of glory is intended as symbolic of this person-to-person, I-Thou relationship.

And here **is** our comfort: to know that neither death (whether our own or that of a loved one), nor life, nor angels, nor principalities, nor losses present, nor losses to come, nor powers, nor height, nor depth of depression, nor any grief in all creation, will be able to separate us from the love of God in Christ Jesus our Lord.

canto viii

"Blissful," quod I, "may this be true?
Be not displeased if I speak error.
Art thou the queen of heaven's blue
To whom this world shall all do honor?
We believe in Mary from whom grace grew,
Who bore a bairn ⌐ of virgin flower;
The crown from her who might remove
But one who surpassed her in some favor?
Now, for singularity of the sweetness in her,
We call her Phoenix of Araby,
Who flawless flew from her Fashioner
Like to the Queen of Courtesy."

"COURTESY" becomes the link word for this canto; but we
need to know that the word was much richer in meaning for
the poet than it is for us. For him, "courtesy" was not
simply "elementary politeness." He knew (as likely we do
not) that "courtesy" is built upon the word "court." And
as we hardly could, he knew the royal court as the symbol
and perhaps even demonstration of the highest sort of no-
bility, dignity, graciousness, and benevolence. And
"courtesy" identifies behavior of a courtly sort.

Our poet--along with scripture itself--appreciated the
propriety of God being described as King and of "the kingdom of God" as being his court. And whether we prefer
monarchical government or not, we must learn to **think** in
those terms if we are to have any chance of understanding
either the poet or scripture.

With this "courtly" canto, then, begins an extended
treatment of a central theme: both "the body of Christ" and
"the court of God" are marked by a unique courtesy in which
all are honored without distinction. There are no ranks;
there is no dividing up into honorees and honorers. Don't
confuse this idea with "equality," our modern **democratic**
concept of each individual looking out to make sure he gets
his **rights,** his fair share. Both the poet and scripture
were way out in front of this one; and perhaps "community
of grace" is the best term for their ideal.

The poet applies the theme particularly to the infant's status in glory rather than to the grief of the
father--yet this is not necessarily a digression.

As we have noted, grief tends to center in a feeling
of having been cheated: "I have not received the happiness
that is mine **by right."** But as quickly will be made clear,
the courteous community of God is not and cannot be estab-
lished on the basis of **rights;** it subsists solely in **grace.**
And in the grace of God there are absolutely no grounds for
anyone to complain of being cheated. Here, then, is a very
pertinent answer to grief: **"**You have **not** been cheated!" So
the following stanzas will speak, on the one hand, to the
daughter's **undeserved** honor, but on the other and just as
pointedly, to the father's sense of **undeserved** loss.
"Community of grace" leaves no room for concepts of either
"high" or "low."

VIII : 2

"Courtesy's Queen!" the girl then said,
Kneeling to ground and covering her face,
"Matchless mother and merriest maid,
Blessed beginner of every grace!"
Then rose she up and did upbraid
And speak against me in short space:
"Sir, many here seek and are repaid
But supplanters are none within this place.
That Empress all the heavens doth grace;
And earth and hell are her levy.
She from her heritage none will chase,
For she is Queen of Courtesy.

VIII : 3

"The court of the kingdom of God alive
A property hath in its self-being:
All that may therein arrive
Of all the realm is queen or king
And yet shall never another deprive;
But each one is glad of others' having,
And would their crowns were thus
                                    worth five,
If possible were such enhancing.
But my Lady, of whom Jesus did spring,
She holds the empire o'er us full free;
And none is displeased of our gathering,
For she is Queen of Courtesy.

VIII : 4

"Through courtesy, sayeth Saint Paul,
We all are members of Jesus Christ.
As head and arms and legs and all
Tie into his body full true and tried,
Right so is every ⌐ Christian soul
A legitimate limb of the Master of Might.
Then look whether hate or any gall
Is attached or tied thy limbs betwixt;
Thy head feels not jealousy nor jaundice
On arm or finger a bangle to see;
So fare we all with love and bliss
As king and queen by courtesy."

"Courtesy," quod I, "I do believe;
And may charity great be you among.
But that my speech may not you grieve

  *   *   *   *   *   *   *   *

Thyself in heaven over high you heave
To make thee queen that was so young!
What greater honor might he achieve
Who hath endured in the world as strong
And lived in penance his whole life long
With bodily bale him bliss to buy?
What more honor might to him belong
Than being crowned king by courtesy?

THERE IS A LINE missing in the original manuscript; and because that manuscript is our sole source for the poem, there would seem no chance of ever recovering it. The likelihood is that the copyist accidentally skipped a line in his copying. Nevertheless, he will have been saved by grace--as must we all be for the lines **we've** skipped.

The Jeweler now shows himself to be very much one of us. We are all so hooked on the human order of "rights," "deserts," and "deservings" that we can't accept the astonishing "community of grace" as being somehow quite **fair.** "Sure, heavenly blessings are great; but--I don't know--it sort of takes the edge off to know that everybody else gets the same thing." Grace takes some getting used to. And so the Jeweler now finds himself caught in a turnabout that has him arguing that his "peerless pearl" has been given a "peerage" higher than he actually had in mind for her. And in just such contradiction is where we wind up when we choose to go the route of "rights."

CANTO IX

"That courtesy is too free of deed,
If it be so what thou dost say.
Thou livest not two years in our glebe;
Thou couldst not God either please nor pray,
Nor ever knew either Pater nor Creed,
And made a queen the very first day?
I cannot believe ～ so God me speed! ～
That God would wander so wrong away.
As *countess*, damsel, by my faith,
'Twere fair in heaven that far to climb,
Or else a lady of less array ～
But a queen? That is too dear a time!"

IX : 2

"There is no 'time' to his goodness,"
Then said to me that worthy wight,
"For all is truth in his largesse
And he may nothing do but right.
As Matthew mentions in your mass,
In truthful Gospel of the God of Might,
An example ∠ he can full easily assess
And liken it to heaven's light:
'My kingdom,' he sayeth, 'is like on high
To a lord who had a vineyard fine,
Where the season of year to term was nigh
That vineyard labor was dear of time.

IX : 3

"That time of year well know these servants.
The lord full early up he rose
To hire workmen for his vineyard
And findeth there some for his purpose.
Into accord they could incline
For a penny a day; and forth the group goes,
Twisting and toiling at cost of great pain
To cut and carry and bind the crop close.
Later to market the lord again goes
And findeth men whiling the time away.
"Why standeth ye idle?" he sayeth to those,
"Know ye not what is the time of day?"

IX : 4

""Ere it was daytime, hither we'd come,"
So all the same was the answer he sought.
"We've been standing here since up
                                rose the sun,
And no man at all bids us do aught."
"Go into my garden; do what ye can,"
So saith the lord, making it taut.
"What reasonable hire may be run up
I will pay you in deed and in thought."
Into the vineyard they went and they wrought.
All thru the day the lord was steadfast;
And new men to his vineyard he brought
Until the daytime well-nigh was passed.

IX : 5

"'That day, at time of evensong,
An hour before the sun goes down,
He yet ∟ saw idle men full strong
And saith to them with sober sound,
"Why stand ye idle this whole day long?"
They said their hire was nowhere found.
"Go to my vineyard, yeomen young,
And work and do whate'er ye might."
Soon all the world nestled toward night;
The sun was down, and it waxed late.
To take their hire did he invite;
The day was all a time past date.

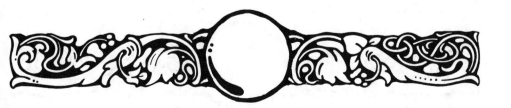

canto x

" 'The time of day the Lord did know,
Called to the reeve, "Lad, pay the men.
Give them the hire that I them owe.
And further ~ that none may e'er

reprove ~

Set thou them all upon a row,
And give each one alike a penny.
Start with the last who standeth low
Till to the first thou doth attain."
And then the first began a plaint
And said that they had travailed sore,
"These but one hour themselves did strain;
We think we ought to take the more.

X : 2

" ' "More have we served, we thinketh so,
Who suffered have the day's fierce heat,
Than 𝔏 those who wrought not hours two;
Yet thou doth them to us equate!"
Then saith the lord to one of those:
"Friend, I'll not concede I did thee cheat.
Take what is thine own and go.
If hired for a penny agreed,
Why shouldst thou now become aggrieved?
Wast not a penny thy covenant before?
Further than covenant there's naught
                                        to plead.

Why shouldst thou then ask me for more?

X:3

"""More: is it not lawful with my gift,
To do with mine whate'er seems meet?
Dost thou thine eye to lust now lift,
Because I'm good and no one cheat?"
"Thus shall I," quod Christ, "it sift:
The last shall be the first I greet,
And the first the last, be he ne'er so swift
For many be called tho few get the mark.""
Thus poor men always possess their part,
Though they come last as inferior
Or at swinging scythes do only start,
The mercy of God is much the more.

"More's mine of joy and bliss herein,
Of ladyship great and life of light,
Than all the wights in the world might win
Who ask for judgement according to right
Though only this moment I didst begin!
To be hired at eventide wast my plight;
Yet, first, for my hire the Lord called me in,
The whole and the sum paid me outright.
Yet others there were who'd more time put in,
Who'd sweltered and sweat long years
                              before,
Who still of their hire nothing have seen,
Perchance this year will see nothing more."

X:5

Then more mouthed I and spoke so pert:
"Methink thy tale unreasonable;
God's right is ready, and it he'll assert,
Or else Holy Writ is but a fable.
In the Psalter is a verse ⊻ overt
That speaketh a point determinable:
'Thou requitest according to each his desert,
Thou high King ever indomitable.'
Now he who stood the long day stable,
If *thou* to payment came him before,
Then thou, less in work, to take more

art able,

And ever longer the less, the more!"

canto xi

"Of more & of less where God doth rule keep,"
That gentle one said, "there is no regard;
For everyone there his full pay doth reap
Whether little or much be his reward.
For the gentle Chieftain is not cheap,
Whether he dealeth mild or hard;
He lavisheth gifts as draughts from
                                    the deep,
Or, in a gulf, gushers that never retard.
One's franchise is large who in faith
                                    is forward
Toward him who doth man's sin rebuff;
No better bliss from him's harbored,
For the grace of God is great enough.

IT WOULD SEEM that both Jesus' parable of the laborers in the vineyard and the Pearl Maiden's argument are meant to address the word of comfort two ways. The "poor men" (those who, as the maiden herself, have nothing to show from life) always, we are told, their part possess, though they come last and are the least. That's a comfort not to be found in this world.

But also, to those who (as the Jeweler) feel that their suffering amounts to work in the vineyard for which they are owed, there comes the word: "You've jeoparded nothing. Each one is fully paid. The gentle Chieftain is not cheap. He lavisheth gifts. No better bliss from you is harbored." And this, too, is a comfort not found in this world—the guarantee that one will never be cheated.

And yet Jesus observed: "Truly, I say to you, the tax collectors and the harlots go into the kingdom of God before you" (Mt. 21:31). The poor come in gladly; but those of us who righteously have been twisting and toiling through the day's fierce heat, we would rather retain our grief—with its sense of "offended deserving"—than come to the comforts of grace on a par with tax collectors and harlots.

Yet let us take care to define these "poor" who come in; the line may not fall where we think it does. We have been careful in our day to school our minorities and disadvantaged in the consciousness-raising of "offended deserving" and "standing up for your rights." These, then, do not come as "the poor in spirit." No, they come as we do, claiming and even demanding their right to God's comfort and restitution. Are there any left who come in the true poverty of "Lord, be merciful to me, a sinner"? That word is not often heard among us anymore.

"But enough now thou speakest, me to berate,
That I my penny wrongly took here;
Thou sayest that I came too late,
Unworthy am to be a peer.
Where knewest thou ever a person abate ~
Ever so holy in his prayer ~
Who never forfeited in some way
The meed some times of heaven's cheer?
And always more often the older they were
They left the right and from it did slough.
Mercy and grace had them then to steer,
For the grace of God is great enough.

XI : 3

"But enough of grace hath the innocent.
As soon as they are born, by line,
In the water of baptism they descend;
Then brought they are to work the vines.
Anon, the day of dark intent
In droop of death makes them decline
Who ne'er wrought wrong ere thence
                                    they went.

Then payeth his help the Lord divine;
They did his behest as they were assigned.
Why shouldn't their work be accepted as such?
Yes, and they be paid at first and in fine?
For the grace of God ‿ is great enough.

XI : 4

"Enough 'tis known that mankind great
First knew bliss untouched by blight;
Our forefather then did it forfeit
Through the apple he did bite.
In his damnation came our fate
To die in dole outside delight,
Then wend our way to hell of hate,
Therein to dwell without respite.
But thereon quickly things came right;
Rich blood ran on a rood so rough
And precious water at that plight;
The grace of God waxed great enough.

XI : 5

"Enough there waxed out of that well
Blood and water from broad wound
The blood bought us from bale of hell
And delivered us from death second.
The water is baptism, truth to tell
Following the javelin so grimly ground
That washes away the guilt so fell
With which Adam us in death hath
                                    drowned.
Now is there nought in this world round
'Twixt us and bliss but what He did rebuff
And what's restored on that hallowed
                                    ground;
And the grace of God is great enough.

canto xii

"Grace enough that man may have
Who sins anew, if he repent;
But with sorrow and sighing he
　　　　　　　　　　　must it crave
And abide the pain that is consequent.
But by reason of right that none will waive,
Saved evermore is the innocent.
It is a judgement God never gave
That the guiltless to damnation be sent.
The guilty one may contrition present
And, through mercy, to grace take flight;
But he who toward guile hath never bent,
As innocent is safe and right.

XII : 2

"Right, thus, I know 'tis in this case,
Two kinds God saveth by his skill:
The righteous man shall see his face;
The faultless fellow come to him still.
The Psalter ℒ says thus in a passage:
'Lord, who shall climb up thy high hill,
Or rest within thy holy place?'
Himself to answer quickly will:
'Who with harmful hands hath not done ill,
Who is of heart both clean and light.'
He shall step in stable style;
The innocent's ever safe by right.

XII : 3

"The righteous man also, for certain,
He shall approach that pretty pile,
Who taketh not his life in vain
Nor gouges his neighbor thru any guile.
Regarding such a one, Solomon saw plain,
How Wisdom doth him honor compile;
By ways full straight she'd him constrain
And show him the kingdom of God awhile,
As one who saith, 'Lo, yon lovely isle!
Thou mayest it win if thou be sprite.'
Yet assuredly, without peril,
The innocent is saved ∽ by right.

XII : 4

"Regarding the righteous yet saith someone
David in Psalter, if e'er thou it spied
'Lord, 'gainst thy servant judgement
                              bring none;
There's no one living 'fore thee justified.'
Thus, to court when thou shalt come,
Where all our causes shall be tried,
Allege thy right, thou mayest be undone
By this very speech I have applied.
Yet he who on that red rood died,
Whose hands the nails did cruelly smite,
Give thee to pass when thou art tried
By innocence and not by right.

IT IS TRULY AMAZING (amazing grace) to find coming out of medieval Roman Catholicism as radical a teaching of salvation by grace as we've just witnessed—and that something more than a century before Martin Luther and the Protestant Reformation could have been of any help. That the poet spends this much detail and emphasis upon his argument is proof enough that he sees it as running against the theological current of his day. He apparently could read his New Testament as well as Luther could his. And perhaps the teaching comes through with that much more force and purity for the fact that it is not the product of one of our Protestant churches—Protestant churches founded on the premise of "salvation by grace" but within which we aren't really sure we want to give up all claim to the penny we know good and well we've **earned**, that is ours **by right**.

But retrace the poet's thought. Writing when he did, he probably had to argue the true innocence of infants at greater length than we would find necessary. We are well enough convinced on that one.

Yet he goes on to insist, with good scriptural support, that such childlike innocence (righteousness) must be the mark of **everyone** who comes in. Thus he picks up on the great biblical demand for holiness and ethical living—and in the process apparently heads directly back into works-righteousness (as frequently seems to be the case within the New Testament itself).

But then, with the present stanza, it all comes together. Yes, only the righteous can come in. However, that requisite righteousness is simply unattainable by us, on our own—"there's no one living 'fore thee justified." So if thou wouldst come alleging thy innocence **as a right**, thou mayest (in fact, thou **willst**) be undone; you have no **right** to Christian comfort and blessing.

However, there is One who on the red rood died and who can and will **give thee** innocence (give thee of **his** innocence)—if thou wilt accept it as "grace" rather than as "right."

And so, the poem will continue, we can come into the kingdom only as children—only as did the Pearl Maiden herself. We must have that quality of innocence and purity; yes. But no more than it is with children is it with us an innocence of **our** achieving, of **our** merit, an innocence that gives **us** any sort of right. No, ours (as theirs) must be the innocence that is the gift of grace. This is the way to the kingdom; and this is the only way to Christian comfort.

XII : 5

"Whoever rightwisely now can read,
Look in the Book and be aware
How Jesus walked the ancient mead
And folk their bairns all to him bear
For hap and health that from him proceed;
To touch their kin they pray him fair.
His disciples, with blame, would them
impede
And with their reasons full many o'erbear;
But Jesus bids them have a care:
'Make way! The children to me I invite;
Such to the kingdom of heaven are heir.'
The innocent ever are safe by right.

canto xiii

"Jesus called to him the mild,
And said this realm no wight might win
Unless he came right as a child,
Else never more he'd come therein.
Harmless, true, and undefiled,
No fleck or flaw of soiling sin
When such knock at the domicile,
Quick for them the gate's unpinned.
There's the bliss that cannot end,
Which the jeweler sought throughout
                              the world,
Sold all his goods, both wool and linen,
To buy himself the flawless pearl.

YOU WILL NOTICE that the opening catch line of this stanza
fails to catch up the link word, "right." That was the
poet's slip-up, not mine--although he obviously knew his
salvation would be by grace and not by "right" (whether one
he earned or the one he missed).

With this stanza a transition is made from the topic
of salvation by grace to Jesus' parable about the pearl of
great price--though, truth to tell, I had never before understood that the "all his **goods**" the merchant sold consisted of wool and linen; but it makes sense. The poet
takes the opportunity to return to a theme he had touched
upon earlier, namely that one's highest value should be a
pure and innocent relationship to Jesus Christ.

"This matchless pearl, when bought,
                      is dear
The jeweler giving all his goods.
'Tis like the realm of heaven clear
So saith the Father of field and flood
For it is spotless, clean, and clear,
Endlessly round and blithe of mode,
And common to all who righteous were.
Lo, it upon my breast has stood!
My Lord the Lamb who shed his blood
In token of peace did it confer.
Forsake the witless world thou should.
And buy thyself a flawless pearl."

XIII : 3

"O flawless pearl in pearls pure,
Who beareth," quod I, "the pearl of price,
He who formed thy fair figure,
Who wrought thy weeds, he was full wise.
Thy beauty came ne'er of nature;
Pygmalion ne'er painted thy visage;
Nor did Aristotle's literature
Describe by kind such properties.
Thy color passes the fleur-de-lis;
Thine angel-manner's so courteous
Brief me, bright one: what kind of office
Beareth the pearl that's so flawless?"

XIII : 4

"My matchless Lamb with whom none compete,"
Quod she, "my dearest Destiny,
Chase me to make his, though hardly meet
That union earlier seemed to be.
When I went from your world's conceit,
He called ∽ me to his felicity,
'Come here to me, my lover sweet,
For mote nor spot there's none in thee.'
He gave me might and yet beauty;
In his blood my wardrobe white he furled
And crowned me, clean in virginity,
And plied me with his flawless pearls."

"Why, flawless bride, who bright doth flame,
Who royalty hath so rich and rife,
What kind of being must be that Lamb
That he would thee wed for his wife?
O'er others all so high dost thou climb
To lead, with him, such ladylike life,
While more comely women under comb
For Christ have lived amongst much strife.
And thou these dears away didst drive
And thru that marriage all others depress
Thyself alone, so staunch and stiff,
A matchless maid and thus flawless!"

THE POOR JEWELER, he just cannot get through his head an understanding of the divine commonality of honor in the community of grace. For him—as for us—you simply do not have honor except in contrast to the lesser status of others. Yet, surely, this divine commonality lies at the very heart of what Christian comfort is all about.

From this point on, the poem will be largely governed by imagery from the Apocalypse, or what we commonly know as the book of Revelation. And I am of the opinion that the poet displays a surprisingly uncommon understanding of that book. His is a very positive, Christocentric interpretation—as over against the usual emphases on punishment, fear, judgment, monstrosity, and crystal-ball calendarizing.

canto xiv

"Flawless," quod that merry queen,
"Unblemished am I, without a blot;
And that in majesty I maintain;
But 'matchless queen' then said I not.
The Lamb's brides in bliss we've been,
A hundred and forty four thousand
                                        flock,
As in the Apocalypse 'tis seen.
Saint John saw them all in a knot
On the hill of Zion, that seemly spot;
The apostle saw them in ghostly dream,
Arrayed for wedding on that hilltop,
The new city of Jerusalem.

XIV: 2

"Of Jerusalem in speech I spell.
If thou wouldst know what kind he be —
My Lamb, my Lord, my dear Jewel,
My Joy, my Bliss, my Lover free —
The prophet Isaiah of him did tell
Piteously of his debonairity,
That glorious guiltless one men did quell
Without any reason of felony.
As sheep to the slaughter there led
                                    was he
And as lamb the shearer takes in hand,
So closed he his mouth to each query
When the Jews judged him in Jerusalem.

XIV : 3

"In Jerusalem was my lover slain
And rent on the rood amongst boys bold.
All our bale to bear full benign,
He took on himself our cares so cold.
With buffets was his face flayed,
Which once so fair was to behold.
For sin he set himself in vain,
Who ne'er by it had been controlled.
For us, himself was flogged and flailed,
And broken upon a boisterous beam.
As meek as a lamb that no plaint told
For us he died in Jerusalem.

: XIV : 4

"Jerusalem, Jordan, and Galilee ~
There, as baptised the good Saint John,
His words with Isaiah's did agree.
When Jesus then toward him had gone,
He spoke of him this prophesy:
'Lo, God's Lamb, as ∠ true as stone,
Who doth for the sins stand warranty
Which all this world hath wrought upon.'
Of himself surely he wrought none,
Yet on himself took all the stain.
His generation, who can reckon,
Who died for us in Jerusalem?

THE POET, it would seem, has correctly located and interpreted the "Jesus as Lamb" symbol according to the understanding of the early Christian tradition itself—spotting it, as he does, in the 53rd Chapter of Isaiah, in John the Baptist's statements in the opening chapters of the Gospel of John, and finally, in Revelation.

This meditation on the suffering and the atoning death of Jesus is very appropriate to the theme of Christian comfort. Merely to get our attention off our own suffering and onto his is a great gain. In the face of the cross, self-centeredness has to begin to give way.

More, in the cross we are confronted with the fact of how much we are loved and cared about, how much God has shown himself willing to give even for the sake of those who wrongly accuse him of having cheated them. It is hard to stand at the foot of the cross and call the Chieftain cheap.

Finally and perhaps most important, after the cross, it is impossible anymore to think of the God whom we address in our grief as being merely the worker of that grief, the observer of that grief. No, now we must admit that our sufferings have pained him more than they have us; our griefs have grieved him more truly than they have us. The Lord is the man of sorrows and acquainted with grief (while we have resisted grief and refused its positive acquaintance). In the face of the cross, then, we must know that he has been **with** us in suffering. So if there is antagonism, it can be only because we have been **against** him, rather than he against us.

XIV : 5

"In Jerusalem thus my lover sweet
Twice for a lamb was taken there
By record true of either prophet,
For his mode so meek and his way so fair.
The third time is thereto full meet,
In the Apocalypse 'tis written clear:
Amidst the & throne 'round which
                                saints took seat,
The Apostle John saw him right there,
Opening the book with pages square
Where seven signets were set in line.
And at that sight all froze in fear ~
In hell, in earth and Jerusalem.

canto xv

"This Jerusalem Lamb had never a patch
Of other hue than brilliant white,
On which no spot nor stain could stretch,
The white wool was so rich and rife.
Therefore each soul that had ne'er a touch
Is for that Lamb a worthy wife.
And though each day a store he fetch,
Among us comes neither struggle nor strife;
But each one singly would we were five—
The more the merrier, so God me bless!
In company great, our love doth thrive
In honor more and never the less.

XV:2

"To less of bliss may none us bring
Who bear this pearl upon our breast;
For they on mischief ne'er could think
Who wear spotless pearls all in a crest.
Although our corpses in the clods cling
And thou art raving in rue without rest,
Throughout we all still have our knowing:
To one death our hope is full addressed.
On the Lamb who glads us our care is cast;
With mirth his love-feast doth us bless;
Each one's bliss is biggest and best,
Yet no one's honor ever the less.

THE DAUGHTER, "a corpse that in the clods clings."

The father "raving in rue without rest."

Yet "to one death our hope is full addressed."

A tremendous insight.

The daughter knows that her physical death was of no ultimate significance. Sooner or later it had to take place; she was, at best, a rose that flowers and fails.

The father **thinks** his dying to happiness, his raving in rue, does have significance--as proof of his offended innocence and a work that makes him deserving of consolation and restitution. He is wrong.

To **one** death our hope is full addressed. It is only that voluntary, vicarious death on the cross that has any ultimate significance, for all other deaths are caught up, canceled out, and redeemed in that one. And it is only when the Jeweler can get past the death of his daughter, past the death of his own happiness, and get centered onto this death of God--it is only then that true comfort will make itself felt.

XV : 3

"Lest thou my tale find less than sound,
In the Apocalypse 'tis written so:
'I saw,' says John, 'the Lamb take stand
On the Mount of Zion in glory aglow
And with him maidens a hundred thousand
And four and forty thousand also.
On all their foreheads written I found
The Lamb's and his Father's names in

                        a row.

A hue from heaven I then heard too
Like welling waters running in rush
And thunder rolling through mountains blue.
The loudness, I think, had never been less.

XV : 4

"Nonetheless, though it shouted sharp,
And litany loud although it were,
A note full new I heard sound forth;
To listen to it was lovely dear!
As harper harping on his harp
That new song now they sang full clear,
In sonorous notes, a gentle carp.
Full fair the modes of melody were
Right before our God's great chair
And the four beasts that him profess
And the elders of mien demure,
Their song they sang nevertheless.

"'Nevertheless, none's e'er had a throat
For all the crafts that ever they knew
That they of that song might sing a note,
Except those of the Lamb's retinue;
For they alone from the earth are bought
As firstfruits which to God are due.
To the gentle Lamb are they betrothed,
Like to himself in looks and hue;
For never a lie nor tale untrue
E'er touched their tongues in any distress.'
That cleansed company can never remove
From its matchless Master, nevertheless!"

XV : 6

"Nevertheless my pardon grant,"
Quod I, "my pearl, though I questions pose;
I should not flout thy reflections frank,
Whom Christ for his bridal chamber chose.
I'm mingled with muck and mold so dank;
And thou art so rich, a resplendent rose
Abiding here on this blissful bank
Where love of life one cannot lose.
Now, gracious, who simplicity doth enclose,
I would ask of thee a thing express;
And though I'm a bumpkin so verbose,
Let my prayer prevail nevertheless.

THIS CANTO, it so happens, has **six** stanzas. That could be because an interpolator at some point inserted an extra (although which of the six it might be is by no means evident). It could be that the poet simply lost count; the writing of the poem had to involve keeping track of any number of things at the same time. It could be that the poet wanted to show the poem who is master; if he wants an extra stanza, he'll put it in.

Nevertheless, notice the stanza's first line; he does beg our pardon.

CANTO XVI

"Nevertheless, upon thee I call ~
If thou canst see to its being done ~
Since thou art glorious, without gall,
Withhold never this plea of my own.
Have ye no dwelling in castle wall,
No manor that ye can call home?
Thou tellest of Jerusalem, the realm
                                    royal

Where David dear was placed on throne;
But in these woods it ne'er was known;
But in Judea 'tis, that noble abode.
As ye are spotless under the moon,
So should your home be without mote.

WITH THIS CANTO, the poet has thrown a curve I cannot handle. The new link word he here introduces is "mote." No problem. From the Anglo-Saxon there had come into English the word "mote," meaning "a speck or flaw." Thus we read in Matthew 6:3 KJV, "And why beholdest thou the **mote** that is in thy brother's eye, but considerest not the beam that is in thine own eye?"

However, as chance (or mischance) would have it, from the French there had also come into English another word "mote," meaning, originally, a mound or hill. Later (and with our poet) it came to mean a city or fortress set on a hill. Still later it came to designate such a fortress **surrounded by water.** And finally it became "moat," identifying the water barrier itself.

But our oh-so-clever poet chose to use both "motes" as his link word, moving freely from one to the other. And thus for us to attempt a translation of either word would be to lose the linkage altogether. However, if the poet's original readers were smart enough to read the word one way or the other, I guess you are, too. But be prepared for him to describe the new Jerusalem as "the mote without a mote." And of course, "moteless" is to be read "flawless."

"This moteless band of which thou dost tell,
Of thousands thronged, so great a rout,
So many ye be, a great citadel
Ye must have, without a doubt.
So comely a pack of jolly jewels,
'Twere ill that they should lie without.
And where I tarry in this dell
(I see no buildings hereabout)
I trow alone ye wend in and out
To look on the glory of this graceful
                              growth.
If thou hast other lodgings stout,
Now show to me that merry mote."

XVI : 3

"The mote thou meanest in Judah-land,"
That special spirit then to me spake,
"That's the city the Lamb had planned
To suffer in sorely for man's sake ~
The ℒ old Jerusalem, ye understand;
For there old guilt was finally slaked.
But the new, here alighted at God's

command,

The apostle in Apocalypse as theme did take.
The Lamb there without spots black
Hath now fetched thither his fair drove;
And as his flock is without fleck,
So is his mote without a mote.

"Of motes two, to cut it clean,
And both called Jerusalem naytheless ~
To you that is to say, I ween,
'City of God' or 'Vision of Peace.'
For making our peace one was the scene;
In pain to suffer the Lamb it chose.
In the other is nothing but peace to glean
That ever shall last and never foreclose.
That is the town toward which we close
From the time our flesh by death is smote;
There glory and ⌐ bliss forever grows
For the company without a mote."

XVI : 5

"Moteless maid with majesty mingling,"
Then said I to that lovely flower,
"Bring me to that beautiful building,
And let me see that blissful bower."
Said she, "That God will to nothing bring;
Thou mayest not enter within his tower.
But, for thee, of the Lamb I've asked
                                        this thing,
For sight thereof, through great favor.
Without to see ⟨ that clean closure
Thou mayest; but within, not a foot
To stretch in the street hast thou vigor,
Unless thou wert clean, without a mote.

canto xvii

"If I shouldst this mote to thee unhide,
Bend thy way up to this brook's head;
And I, anent thee on this side,
Shall follow till thou seest a hill bestead."
Then would I no longer 'bide
But lurched thru lindens lovely leaved
Till on a hill I it espied
And sighted the city as forth I moved,
Beyond the brook where low I stood.
Brighter than with shafts of sun it shone;
In Apocalypse is its fashion proved,
As described it is by the Apostle John.

: XVII : 2

As John the Apostle saw the sight,
I saw that city of great renown,
Jerusalem so new and royal bedight,
As it from heaven had alighted down.
The city was all of spotless gold bright,
As gleaming glass that's burnished
                              all 'round,
With gentle gems beneath set tight.
Twelve tiers at the base bound
The twelve foundations do richly compound.
Each tier was a separate stone,
As dearly described is this very town
In Apocalypse by the Apostle John.

Since John these stones in writing did name,
I knew the names from his account:
Jasper 'tis called, the first of gems
That on the first base I found out ⌒
It glistened green on the lowest course.
Sapphire was the second, no doubt.
Chalcedony then, without weakness,
In the third table was pearly pale.
The emerald was fourth, so green of scale.
Sardonyx was ⌐ the fifth stone.
The sixth, the ruby ⌒ he did it hail
In Apocalypse, did the Apostle John.

Yſet joined John the chrysolite,
The seventh gem in the fundament;
The eighth, the beryl clear and white.
Topaz, twin-hued, in ninth was set.
Chrysoprase the tenth bedight.
Jacinth the eleventh ennobled.
The twelfth ⁓ the gentlest in every light ⁓
Was purple amethyst with indigo blent.
Above the tiers the battlements bent,
Of jasper as glass that glistening shown.
I knew it by his devisement
In the Apocalypse of the Apostle John.

: XVII :5

As John divined, yet saw I there
That these twelve tiers were like a stair.
The city stood above four square,
As long, as broad, ∽ as high, full fair.
The streets of gold were as glass all bare.
The walls of jasper did glint and glare.
The wainscotings within adorned were
With all precious stones that they could
                                    bear.
Then held each line of the city square
To twelve furlongs as it ran on
In height, in breadth, in length given o'er,
For so saw it measured the Apostle John.

canto xviii

As John him writes, more came to sight:
Each plane of that place, it had three
                                    gates.

So twelve in succession I espied,
The portals paved in richest plates
And every gate a margarite ~
A perfect pearl that never fades.
On each one was a name inscribed
Of the children of Israel, following
                                    their dates,

That is to say, by their birthdays;
The eldest, thus, was first thereon.
And such light each street illuminates,
There needeth neither sun nor moon.

XVIII : 2

Of sun or moon had they no need;
The self of God was their lamp light,
The Lamb the lantern his folk to lead;
By him shone the city eternally bright.
Thru hearth and home my gaze did speed,
For, subtly clear, naught blocked

the light.

The high throne there then might ye heed,
With all its apparelment bedight
As John the Apostle doth plainly cite.
The high God himself there sits eftsoon;
From the throne a river runs outright,
Brighter than both the sun and moon.

XVIII : 3

Sun or moon shone ne'er so sweet;
Ever that fulgent flood flowed out.
Swiftly it swung through every street,
Without any filth or gall or glut.
A church ∟ therein had been conceit,
As would chapel or temple that e'er was

    built ∼

The Almighty, he was the minister meet,
The Lamb, the sacrifice redeeming debt.
The gates all shut were never yet;
Evermore open they at every zone.
But none entereth there escaping threat
Who bears any spot under the moon.

: XVIII : 4

The moon to encroach there has no might
Too spotty it is, of body too grim.
And also there where is never night,
Why shouldst the moon its compass climb?
Compared to that all worthy light
Which shines upon the brook's fine brim
The planets are in too poor a plight
And the sun itself full far too dim.
Around that water are trees full trim
That twelve fruits of life can bear
                              full soon;
Twelve times a year they bear full limbed
And renew their crop with every moon.

XVIII : 5

Under the moon so great a marvel
No fleshly heart might e'er endure
As when that city my sight did assail.
So fair thereof was its nature,
I stood as ∠ still as a dazed quail
For fascination with that figure.
Felt I neither rest nor travail,
So raptured was I with its gleam full pure.
For I dare say with conscience sure
Had a bodily being 'bided that boon,
Though all the clerks had him in cure,
His life had been lost under the moon.

CANTO XIX

Right as the mighty moon can rise
After the day-gleam's driven down,
So suddenly, in wondrous wise,
I was aware of a procession.
This noble city of rich emprise
Was suddenly full ~ without any

summon~

Of all such virgins in the same guise
As was my blissful one under crown.
And crowned were all of them in that fashion,
Bedecked in pearls and raiment white;
On each one's breast was badged and bound
The blissful pearl beyond delight.

WITH THE PEARL POET, as with the Revelator himself, I would suggest, all the imagery of architectural splendor is but prelude and setting for the picture of **community** into which we now move--the courteous community of the Lamb.

Again the pearl imagery becomes strong, the imagery of purity and pricelessness. The pearl of great price, for which the merchant sold all, has been found. It is, of course, a **singular** gem; it is the Lamb himself, "that gay Jewel!" Yet, even so, it is **plural** as well; "on **each one's** breast was badged and bound the blissful pearl beyond delight." Such is the magic and majesty of the kingdom of God!

XIX : 2

With great delight they glided together
O'er golden streets that gleamed like glass.
Hundreds of thousands, I wot, there were;
And all alike their livery was.
Hard to know whose the gladdest cheer!
The Lamb before did proudly pass
With seven horns ⸜ of red gold clear;
Like prized pearls his raiment was.
Toward the throne they trooped en masse;
Though they were many, no press in

                     the plight;
But mild as maidens seemly at mass,
So drove they forth with great delight.

XIX : 3

The delight his coming now induced,
Too much it were of which to tell.
The elders, then, when he approached,
Prostrate at his feet they ⌇ fell.
Legions of angels, together summoned,
There cast incense of sweet smell.
Then glory and glee anew were broached
All sang to laud that gay Jewel!
The strain might strike thru earth to hell
Which the Virtues of heaven with joy
                                    indite.

To laud the Lamb where his people dwell,
In truth I felt was great delight.

XIX : 4

Delight in striving the Lamb to devise,
With much of marveling, thru my mind went.
Best was he, blithest, and most to prize
Of any upon whom speech is spent⌒
So worthily white were those weeds of his,
His looks so simple, himself eminent!
But a wound full wide ⌒ and wet there is
Anent his heart, thru skin that's rent;
From his white side his blood gave vent.
Alas, thought I, who worked that spite?
Any breast for bale should have
                              felt torment
Ere therein it had had delight.

XIX:5

But the Lamb's delight could none demean;
Though he was hurt and a wound had,
In his semblance it ne'er was seen,
His glances were so gloriously glad.
I beheld then in those he did convene
How they with life were lavished and lade.
Then saw I there my little queen
Methought stood by me in the glade.
Lord, much of mirth it was she made
Amongst her friends who were so white!
The sight made me think that I would wade
For love-longing toward that great
                                    delight.

THE LAMB bears a terrible wound. We all bear wounds; but his is worst. (And notice, now, that the Jeweler has entirely forgotten his.) Yet the Lamb in his joy--his joy over **us**--also forgets his; "in his semblance it ne'er was seen, his glances were so gloriously glad." The writer to the Hebrews (12:2) speaks of Jesus, "who for the **joy** that was set before him endured the cross, despising the shame, and is seated at the right hand of the throne of God."

And once we are willing to look away from our own wounds and look upon his, ours can be forgotten, too. In his wounds our sorrows can be drowned. His heart was broken so that it could receive our broken hearts. And here, then, **is** Christian comfort: "I beheld then in those he did convene, how they with **life** were lavished and lade." There is "much of mirth" in the great delight of knowing that, even with all our wounds, we live together in him.

canto xx

Delight drove o'er me thru eye and ear;
My mortal mind in madness melted.
When I saw my fair one, I would be there
Beyond the water, though she's insulted.
I thought that nothing might interfere
Or fetch me a blow and bring me to halt;
Springing into the stream, naught
                            could me veer
From my intent, whate'er befall.
But of that mind I was forestalled!
When I 'cross the stream wouldst spring
                            without measure,
From that thought I was recalled ⌒
'Twas not in accord with my Prince's pleasure.

NOTE THE CONCLUDING CATCH LINE of this stanza and identify the link word of our final canto, "pleasure." Be aware, also, that the verb "to please," the noun "pleasure," and the adjective "pleasant" are all variations of the same root. Then recall the very first line of the poem: "Pearl, pleasant to a prince's pleasure." We have come full circle—but with what gain! We began by talking (easily enough) about a pearl—that paradoxical product of a wounded oyster—one which any prince or nobleman would have found pleasing. We wind up with the same words but talking about pure and priceless pearl-people who are pleasing to the Prince of Peace. And in such godliness is great gain!

WE ARE BACK NOW, also, to the "deep river" of tradition (song, story, and poem)—there to discover that the poor Jeweler still does not understand. However, the Pearl Poet uses the river to different (and I would say, greater) effect than any other writer I know. Usually the river represents simply the passage of death, whether that takes place in fear or in peace. But our poet uses it to reveal to us something very important about ourselves.

As is the case with the Jeweler himself, our generation (perhaps above all others) is a generation of "Paradise Stormers." Powered by a strong sense of deserving innocence ("I've suffered enough already—that's what the pastor says") we have a **right** to happiness and are not shy about asserting it. We, with the Jeweler, are ready to charge across the stream, come what may: "If she's there, I have a right to be there; it's only fair."

With us, of course, it is not that we are all that eager to get to the River Jordan and beyond. For us, that's not where Paradise lies anymore. No, the one we have an eye on is the Paradise of Here-and-Now; and that we are going to **have**, one way or another. We've had a hard time of it, and we deserve a little comfort.

Obviously "the world" is quick to offer (for a price) all that we need for health and happiness—in some cases with actually **twice** the amount of active ingredients (like, say, **two** aspirins). But now "the church" promises to do you even better; it can give you the same thing for nothing. "Not as the world gives give I unto you—but even cheaper and easier."

And so, in the Conservative Christian Chapel, the visiting Go-Get-'Um-for-Jesus holds forth: "Come unto me all ye that are weary and heavy-laden (yes, we know that hangnails can hurt like anything) and I will give you **instant miracle.** Just come forward with your request (place your order here, please). Jesus wants you happy; so give your life to him, and everything will be hunky-dory in a jiffy." (Meanwhile, in the background, the choir is singing softly: **"When he calls me** I will answer; I'll be somewhere listening for my name.")

Across the street, in the First Liberal Fellow-and-Gal-Ship, the word is: "Now, now, that's all right. We understand. Everybody does something like that once in a while. But we accept you as a **person.** Why don't you sign up for our Christian Stroking Group or come to our class on Tea and Sympathy for the Weary and Heavy-Laden (Hangnails Included)?"

Of course, out in the middle of the street stands Jeremiah, complaining:

> They have healed the wound of my people lightly,
>   saying, "Peace, peace,"
>   when there is no peace.

To which "they who heal lightly and blithely" would have a perfect right to respond: "Don't blame us. We're giving the people what they want--in fact, what they **demand.** You should know they aren't the type who are about to **wait upon the Lord** to renew their strength. They feel they've suffered enough already."

We **are** a generation of Paradise Stormers; and we will wake up right where the Jeweler does.

It pleased him not that I did push
'Cross miraculous margins in mad array.
Though rash and reckless in the rush,
Yet the event itself didst me gainsay.
For, right as down the bank I thrust,
That wrong wrenched my dream agley.
Then wakened I 'mongst the garden's
                                    brush;
And my head upon that hillock lay
Where my pearl to the ground didst stray.
I came to as from a seizure;
And, grieving, to myself didst say:
"Now all be to the Prince's pleasure!"

: XX : 3

I was pleased full ill to be excised
So suddenly from that fair region,
From all those sights so pleasant and
                                    prized.

A heavy longing struck me numb;
And mournfully then I agonized:
"O pearl," quod I, "of rich renown,
So dear it is what thou devised
To show me in veracious vision.
If true and tried this be a sermon
That thy estate is heavenly treasure,
Then 'tis well with me in this dolorous
                                    dungeon
That thou art to the Prince's pleasure."

: XX : 4

To that Prince's pleasure if I'd always bent
And yearned no more than for me was spread
And myself held to that in true intent
As prayed me that pearl who with me pled
Then, disposed & drawn to God's presence,
Into more of his mysteries would I
                              have been led.
But always doth man more happiness hunt
Than might by right be his privilege.
Therefore my joy asunder was rived
And I cast from the castle of endless measure.
Lord, mad are they who 'gainst thee
                              have strived
Or proffered thee aught against thy pleasure.

IF, even in our grief and brokenheartedness, we had been willing to give thought to the Prince's pleasure . . .

IF we had learned contentment with what we had, rather than always yearning for more than for us was spread . . .

BUT always doth man more happiness hunt than might by right be his privilege.

By **right,** we deserve nothing. In Luke 17:10, Jesus tells us, "So you also, when you have done all that is commanded you, say, 'We are unworthy servants; we have only done what was our duty.'"

Yet if we had been willing to accept life at the Prince's pleasure, who can say what comfort might have been ours?

"Lord, mad are they who 'gainst thee have strived—or **proffered** thee aught against thy pleasure!" Our "volunteering" for Paradise has been as presumptuous as our "demanding" comfort on our own terms.

DEAR LORD, FORGIVE!

XX : 5

To please the Prince or with him get right
Easily comes to the good Christian;
For I've found him, both day and night,
A God, a Lord, a Friend full fine.
Upon the hillock I accepted my plight
For pity of the pearl I pine.
Then gave I that pearl to God outright
In blessed memory of the Christ divine
Who, in the form of bread and wine,
The priests do daily show by measure.
To be humble hirelings he doth us assign
And precious pearls unto his pleasure.

amen

amen

An Appendix:
on the translation

THIS TRANSLATION must be categorized both as original and as derivative. It is original in that I worked directly from the original text--not the original manuscript, of course, but from a couple different editions of the text. However, the translation also is derivative in that I make no claim of being a student of Middle English nor of being able to read it straight off. I have depended upon the translations and glossaries of other scholars, even while seldom following their readings.

My translation may be unique in its attempt to preserve as much as possible of the original poem in the process of making it accessible to modern readers. The result is a translation that is both more and less literal than others.

The tendency is for a translator to latch on to one aspect or feature of the poem, preserve that in all possible exactitude, and let happen what may to the other features. Thus, there are prose translations which seek accurately to reproduce the poet's thought in modern English--without regard to meter, rhyme, alliteration, or link words. There is, on the other hand, at least one modern translation (paraphrase) which gets the rhyme and meter all correct but at the cost of the poet's own words, his alliteration, and his linkage. My method, on the contrary, has been that of continual compromise, trading off one feature against another to the end of preserving as much of all of them as is possible.

I have used more of the poet's **exact words** than has any other translation I've seen. Many of his words have changed enough over the centuries that they no longer express to us his meaning as well as more modern words would do. Nonetheless, wherever I felt the reader could follow the general sense and make correction for the differences of overtone, I chose to let the original word stand.

At great pains (and with residual awkwardness) I have completely reproduced the poet's original pattern of catch lines with their link words. I think he considered this an important feature of his work.

Likewise, I think I have preserved almost as much alliteration as is in the original—and in the places where the poet had it. Many times my word is not all that close in meaning to his; but if I could retain his general sense and still alliterate, I did.

Within these parameters, then, I tried to preserve as much of the original rhyme and meter as possible. That preservation is by no means perfect; yet enough has been retained to keep the reader aware that rhyme and meter are (or were) present.

While doing the translation, I became very impressed with the author's way with words, his ability **as a poet**. When writing the commentary, I was struck in a quite different way—by his insight as a Christian theologian and teacher. This writer—of whom we know not so much as his name—was great either way. My prayer is that the effort represented by this book might enable **him** to speak his poetic pearl of Christian counsel for **your** growth and edification.